BLAZE AND THE FOREST FIRE

By C. W. ANDERSON

BILLY AND BLAZE

BLAZE AND THE GYPSIES

BLAZE AND THE FOREST FIRE

BLAZE AND THE FOREST FIRE

By C. W. ANDERSON

NEW YORK · THE MACMILLAN COMPANY   1953

Set up and electrotyped. Published September, 1938
Thirteenth Printing, 1953

BLAZE AND THE FOREST FIRE

Billy was a boy who loved horses more than anything else in the world. He loved his own pony, Blaze, best of all. After his father and mother gave him Blaze, Billy spent most of his time with the pony. Blaze would come whenever Billy called. He seemed to like the rides through the woods or along the roads as much as Billy did. Billy felt sure that Blaze understood him when he talked; and the pony really did seem to understand what Billy said.

Billy's dog, Rex, usually went with them on their rides. But one day he was sick; so Billy's mother kept him at home. It was a beautiful day, and Billy decided to ride along a little winding road. It passed through some woods, and not many people used it. Both Billy and Blaze liked to ride through the woods, because there were so many things to see. They always met rabbits and squirrels and saw many birds. Flowers grew along the way, and the big trees were green and cool after the hot dusty roads. The summer had been very warm, and there had been little rain.

They had gone quite a long way when Blaze suddenly stopped. Billy looked ahead and saw smoke coming out of a pile of dry brush at the side of the road. He knew that it was against the law to build fires in the woods during the dry season. It was not a safe thing to do because of the danger of starting a forest fire.

Even as Billy looked, the flames burst out. He knew that these flames were the beginning of a forest fire unless they could be put out. If a breeze came up and carried the fire to the big pine trees near by, the whole countryside might burn. Not only the grass and trees would be burned. Fences and barns and houses would also go up in flames.

Billy had once seen a place where a forest fire had been. He remembered how bare and black it had looked, with burnt stumps where beautiful trees had been. He knew he must try to save the woods he loved so much. He must go quickly and get help.

The nearest place to go for help was a large farm. It was a long way to this farm by the road, and there was no time to lose. Billy knew they could save much time if they cut across country through the fields. But to reach the first field they would have to jump a high stone wall, higher than anything Blaze had ever jumped. But Blaze seemed to understand that they needed to hurry. He jumped the high wall perfectly.

Then they went on as fast as they could across the wide field. Billy did not need to urge Blaze. The pony was going like the wind. If he could only keep up this speed, they would soon reach the farmhouse. Billy could see it far off in the distance.

In the middle of the field was a brook. There was no bridge and no time to look for a shallow place to cross. "Come on, Blaze," called Billy, and Blaze went even faster than before. The nearer they came to the brook, the wider it seemed. It was too late to stop now. They were right at the water's edge

Blaze made a tremendous leap. Billy could feel how hard he was trying. It seemed that they would surely get over the brook safely.

As they landed, the bank gave way under the pony's hind feet. For a moment Billy thought they would fall back into the brook. But Blaze scrambled up the bank, and Billy held on somehow, his arms around the pony's neck.

In a flash Billy had his feet in the stirrups again; and they were off as fast as the faithful pony could go. Blaze was breathing hard now, but the farmhouse was near.

Suddenly Billy pulled Blaze to a stop. There, right in front of them, was a high wall with barbed wire at the top. He looked both ways but there was no gate in sight. Billy almost gave up, but the thought of the fire sweeping across the countryside was too much. They must go on.

"Just once more, Blaze," he whispered to the pony. Poor Blaze was very tired, but he galloped bravely toward the fence. He was straining every muscle for the jump.

They were almost over when Billy felt Blaze's hind legs catch on the wire, and they began to fall.

Down went Blaze to his knees, and Billy slipped out of the saddle and up on the pony's neck. It seemed certain that Blaze would go down all the way, taking Billy with him.

But, with a great effort, Blaze scrambled to his feet; and Billy, holding on to the pony's neck, stayed on. Then Blaze started at a gallop for the farmhouse, which was just across the field.

They galloped into the farmyard. The farmer and his son hurried over to meet Billy. All out of breath, he told them about the fire. At once they got some things to use in putting it out. Then they climbed into a car and drove off very fast. The farmer's wife quickly telephoned to the neighbors to send all the help they could.

Blaze was covered with sweat and dirt. He was a very tired pony, but he rubbed his nose against Billy and seemed to know that the boy was proud of him.

"You're the best pony in the world, Blaze— the very best!" said Billy, and he felt sure that what he said was true.

The barbed wire had cut Blaze's legs. So the farmer's wife brought warm water and medicine and helped Billy wash the cuts clean and bandage them. They were not deep cuts, and the farmer's wife said she was sure they would soon heal.

Billy and Blaze had a good rest at the farmhouse and something to eat. Then Billy started for home, letting Blaze walk slowly. On the way they met the farmers coming back. They said that they had been able to put out the fire before it did any real harm. They all thanked Billy for what he had done. They made him feel quite grown up. They said nice things about Blaze, too; so Billy was very happy as he rode home.

When Billy got home, his father and mother were waiting for him. The farmer's wife had telephoned to tell them what had happened. Billy's father took some salve and put it on Blaze's cuts so that they would heal more quickly. Blaze got much petting, and had some carrots with his supper. He was very fond of carrots. Billy had some chocolate cake with his supper. He liked that just as much as Blaze liked carrots. Billy's father and mother were very proud of both Billy and Blaze.

One evening, two weeks later, there was a rap at the door. Billy's mother asked him to go and see who was there. It was one of the farmers who had helped put out the fire. He held a big box on which was written "For Billy and Blaze."

Much excited, Billy opened the box. He found a beautiful new bridle, with a silver headband on which was printed one word —BLAZE. The box held also a pair of shining new boots and a fine pair of riding breeches. They were just the right size for Billy. The people of the countryside had bought all these things for him. They wanted to show Billy how grateful they were that he had saved them from a forest fire.

It was hard to sleep that night. It seemed to Billy that daylight would never come. He got up several times to look at the new boots and the beautiful bridle. He wanted to be sure he hadn't dreamed them.

No one else was awake when Billy brought the new bridle down to the stable and put it on Blaze. Even Rex was still asleep. When Billy got into the saddle wearing his new breeches and boots, he felt fine. He was sure he could ride better because he had them on. Blaze arched his neck proudly. Even in the early dawn the silver headband on the new bridle shone brightly. His cuts were all healed; and he felt fine, too. So the two friends started happily off for their early-morning ride.